Curiosity

Ashley Lee

Explore other books at:
WWW.ENGAGEBOOKS.COM

VANCOUVER, B.C.

 WWW.ENGAGEBOOKS.COM

Curiosity: Good Character Traits
Lee, Ashley, 1995 –
Text © 2024 Engage Books
Design © 2024 Engage Books

Edited by: A.R. Roumanis
Design by: Mandy Christiansen

Text set in Myriad Pro Regular.
Chapter headings set in Anton.

FIRST EDITION / FIRST PRINTING

All rights reserved. No part of this book may be stored in a retrieval system, reproduced or transmitted in any form or by any other means without written permission from the publisher or a licence from the Canadian Copyright Licensing Agency. Critics and reviewers may quote brief passages in connection with a review or critical article in any media.

Every reasonable effort has been made to contact the copyright holders of all material reproduced in this book.

LIBRARY AND ARCHIVES CANADA CATALOGUING IN PUBLICATION

Title: Curiosity / Ashley Lee.
Names: Lee, Ashley, author.
Description: Series statement: Good Character Traits

Identifiers: Canadiana (print) 20230446973 | Canadiana (ebook) 20230446981
ISBN 978-1-77878-651-8 (hardcover)
ISBN 978-1-77878-652-5 (softcover)
ISBN 978-1-77878-653-2 (epub)
ISBN 978-1-77878-654-9 (pdf)

This project has been made possible in part by the Government of Canada.

Curiosity

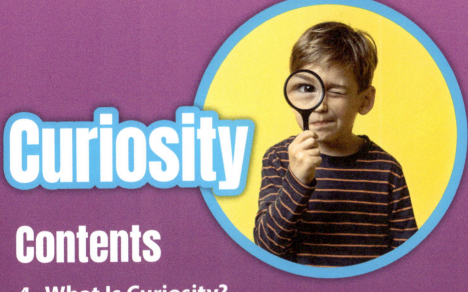

Contents

- 4 What Is Curiosity?
- 6 Why Is Curiosity Important?
- 8 What Does Curiosity Look Like?
- 10 How Does Curiosity Affect You?
- 12 How Does Curiosity Affect Others?
- 14 Is Everyone Curious?
- 16 Is It Bad if You Are Not Curious?
- 18 Does Curiosity Change Over Time?
- 20 Is It Hard to Be Curious?
- 22 How Can You Learn to Be More Curious?
- 24 How Can You Help Others Be More Curious?
- 26 How to Be Curious Every Day
- 28 Curiosity Around the World
- 30 Quiz

What Is Curiosity?

Curiosity is when you want to know more about something.

Curiosity

Curious people like to learn new things.

Why Is Curiosity Important?

Curiosity helps keep your brain **healthy**.

Key Word

Healthy: to be well and not sick.

Curiosity

It makes learning more fun.

What Does Curiosity Look Like?

Curious people ask lots of questions.

Curiosity

They like to **explore** everything around them.

> **Key Word**
> **Explore:** search or look into something.

How Does Curiosity Affect You?

Being curious helps you learn new things.

Curiosity

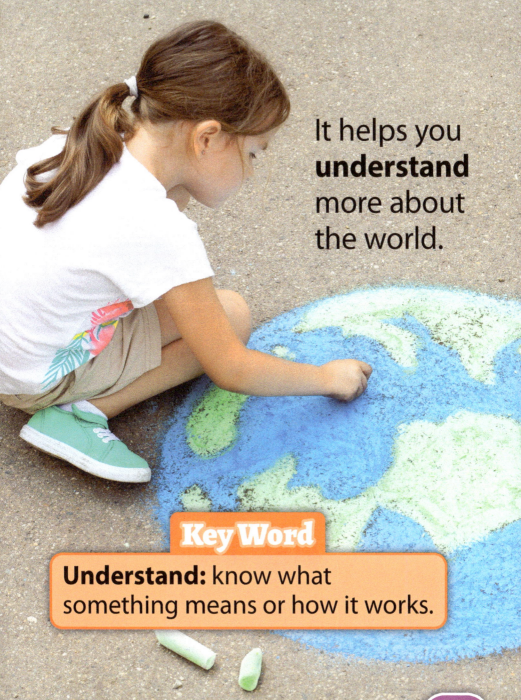

It helps you **understand** more about the world.

Key Word

Understand: know what something means or how it works.

How Does Curiosity Affect Others?

Asking questions can make other people curious too.

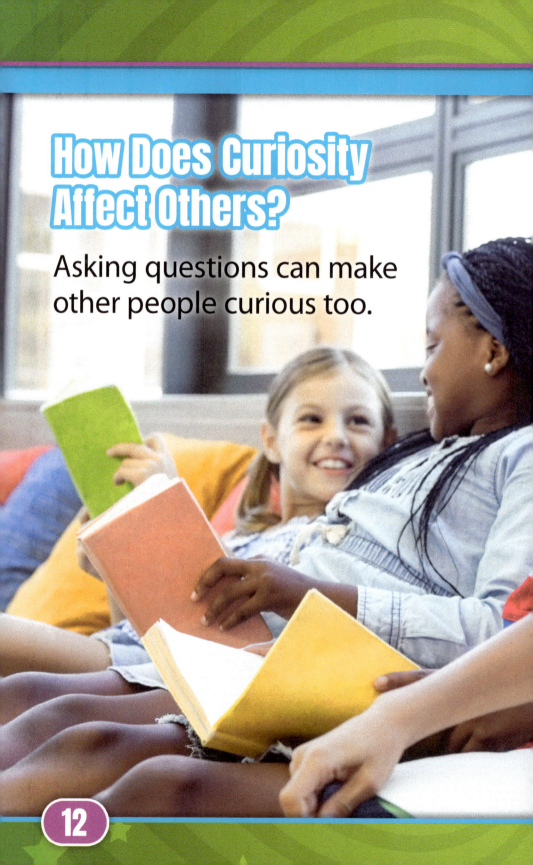

Curiosity

Other people get to learn when you ask questions.

13

Is Everyone Curious?

Sometimes people might not feel curious about something.

Curiosity

That is okay. Everybody is curious about different things.

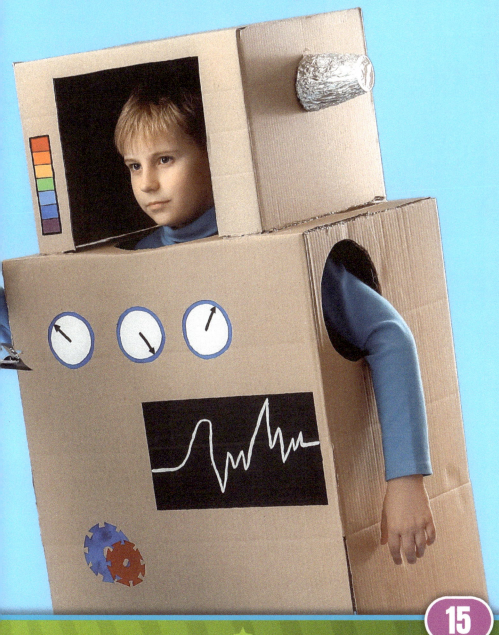

Is It Bad if You Are Not Curious?

It is not bad if you are not curious about something.

Curiosity

People do not have to be curious about everything.

17

Does Curiosity Change Over Time?

Curiosity can grow as you learn more things.

Curiosity

You might become curious about different things as you get older.

Is It Hard to Be Curious?

It can be hard to be curious about things you do not like.

Curiosity

It is easier to be curious about things you do like.

How Can You Learn to Be More Curious?

Think about the things you would like to know more about.

Curiosity

Explore the world outside your home.

23

How Can You Help Others Be More Curious?

Share new things when you learn them.

Curiosity

Ask questions about things other people like.

How to Be Curious Every Day

1. Learn something new every day.
2. Watch what goes on around you.

Curiosity

3. Do not be afraid to say, "I don't know."

4. Ask lots of questions.

Curiosity Around the World

Curiosity helps people **invent** new things every day.

> **Key Word**
> **Invent:** make something new.

Curiosity

Without curiosity, the world would not have lights, TVs, or even books.

Quiz

Test your knowledge of curiosity by answering the following questions. The questions are based on what you have read in this book. The answers are listed on the bottom of the next page.

1 Do curious people like to learn new things?

2 Does curiosity help keep your brain healthy?

3 Does being curious help you learn new things?

4 Is it bad if you are not curious about something?

5 Can curiosity grow as you learn more things?

6 Can it be hard to be curious about things you do not like?

30

Explore Other Pre-1 Readers.

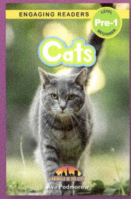
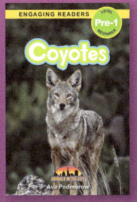

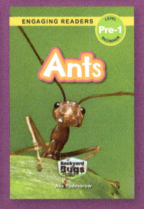

Visit www.engagebooks.com/readers

Answers: 1. Yes 2. Yes 3. Yes 4. No 5. Yes 6. Yes

Milton Keynes UK
Ingram Content Group UK Ltd.
UKHW051105141024
449707UK00017B/195